The Herr

Debbie Robson

abuddhapress@yahoo.com

ISBN: 9798852325389

Debbie Robson 2023

©™®

Alien Buddha Press 2023

In memory of

my grandparents

Bill and Dot Spiller

THE FIRST DAY

The Harbour

From above, looking down on Sydney Harbour, it is an exceptional morning. There is a light breeze that has set white horses dancing on the surface of the harbour but not enough to muddy the breathtakingly deep blue to a dull green. Several ferries have already crisscrossed from north to south before one particular ferry makes its appearance at the Taronga Zoo wharf this October morning in the year 1937. Horns are hooting, waves splashing and as the last passenger boards the ferry, a lion roars. A picture postcard Sydney.

Inside the ferry, the splashing sound subsides. The ferry leaves the wharf and the chugging of the ferry settles into a steady rhythm. Above this sound can be heard high heels on deck. Inside the ferry a young man, looking awkward in his crushed, old fashioned suit, slams a window shut. He takes out a

7

gilt-edged card and looks at it with a confused expression. After a minute he puts the card in his pocket and gazes at the houses through the ferry window. Their existence seems to trouble him; particularly how close they are to the water's edge.

Observing the awkwardness is Roger Maguire. The last thing he needs in his present state of mind is awkwardness. And tension. He'll break the ice, he decides. It always seems to be him breaking the ice but what the hell.

"How about we introduce ourselves? Roger Maguire and you are?"

"John Summers. I'm pleased to meet you. It's very quiet, isn't it?" The young man pulls at his collar as he speaks.

"Yes. Just the two of us."

"No. Three," John pauses. "There's a young woman on deck."

"Is there?" Roger says, feeling a smile plaster his face.

"Yes," John says, stammering as he asks, "But where is everybody else?"

There is the sound of high heels clinking down a steel ramp. Then both men notice pale green shoes, long legs, a floral dress, slim waist and finally an arresting if not beautiful face that exclaims suddenly, "Damn."

Roger tells her, "Watch your step."

"Is there just the three of us?" the young woman asks, looking at both the men as she negotiates the last step into the main seating area and noticing they couldn't be more different – the younger man nervous, the older man urbane.

"It appears so. I'm Roger. This is John."

"I'm Vere. This is the 10 a.m. from Taronga Zoo Wharf, isn't it?"

"Yes, but it's normally a lot busier than this," John comments, sounding a little more confident.

"I missed us setting off. Didn't even see our captain. Been in the head", Roger explains. "Hectic night at the Trocadero."

Vere grimaces but then remarks, "Half your luck. It feels like ages since I've been dancing." She pauses, studying both

9

men. "You must have overdone it," Vere tells Roger.

"Just a tad."

"I've never been to the Trocadero," John says.

"Perhaps not your thing," Vere tells him and softens the comment with a smile.

"No, I love dancing but I have never heard of the place."

"Not heard of the Troc? Where have you been hiding?" Roger asks.

Vere cuts in all business. "Anyway, what does your invitation say? I seem to have left mine at home. On the mantelpiece, I'm pretty sure."

"Now where did I put mine?" Roger pats his pockets. "No joy."

"I have mine."

"Could I have a look, John?"

John passes the invitation to Vere with a shaking hand.

"Thank you."

"Does it have a name on it?" Roger asks, peering over

Vere's shoulder. "I don't think mine did."

"No name. All rather mysterious." Vere pauses and then reads from the gilt-edged card. Catch the 10.00 a.m. Wednesday ferry from Taronga Zoo Wharf and alight at the Hermitage wharf. Celeste and Derek Williams await your arrival." Vere pauses again. "And I mean this isn't the usual ferry and I frankly don't remember a Hermitage wharf."

John takes a deep breath and stammers, "I don't either but then I don't remember this many houses by the water."

"Don't you?" Vere asks.

"And who the hell are Celeste and Derek Williams? Have you met them?" Roger asks.

"No. No. I'm sorry I haven't."

"Nor me," Vere says, taking a cigarette from her handbag. She starts to hunt for a lighter. Both men search their pockets but it is Roger who is first to light Vere's cigarette.

John backs away to look out the nearest window as the ferry chugs along. "Shouldn't we be nearly there? It's before Old

Cremorne Wharf the captain said."

"Did he?" Vere asks.

"Or is it around the point?" Roger asks, throwing the other two into uncertainty.

All three gaze out the window at the small bay ahead, gum trees overhanging the water. A bellbird can be heard just as the ferry engine slows. There is the noise of grating timber.

Suddenly there is a voice from outside. "Well, I haven't got all day. This is the Hermitage, you know."

"Our invisible captain," Roger remarks.

"I'll help tie up," John says and disappears on deck.

"Isn't he keen?" Roger says, lighting a cigarette himself.

"He could probably use some help. I'm going up."

Roger listens to the sound of high heels and a rope being thrown on deck. He expels a long breath, grabs his suitcase and climbs up the stairs. The other two have already collected their luggage from God knows where and are standing on the wharf waiting for him. As he steps off onto the wharf, the ferry immediately heaves clear and toots its horn.

"Well, he is in a hurry," Roger says but the other two aren't listening. They have moved towards a dog that has come pattering down the wharf, barking at their arrival.

"Our welcoming committee," Roger says, as Vere bends down to pat the dog. The sun shines on their shoulders as the three of them walk down the wharf towards land with the golden retriever loping behind.

* * *

The House

In the house a woman in her thirties draws a curtain back and observes the party as they step off the wharf. There has been a mistake, she realises, with one of the party. All three look lost as they survey the grounds of the Hermitage. She closes the curtain to blot them out and moves past a mobile, setting it tinkling.

Bending low, she whispers, "Sweetheart, it's time for a sleep. Shhh. Shhh."

*

From the clouds the all-encompassing sunshine spreads a golden veneer. Beneath the veneer and then below the close canopy of several gum trees, a view of the small party is revealed. Nearby large clumps of pampas grass wave in a light breeze. The men have donned their hats; the woman is bareheaded, her auburn hair catching the light and burnishing it to red.

14

Roger is standing with a proprietorial air next to Vere, John a little behind them under a small gum tree with the luggage. All three are gazing up at the stone staircase that zigzags its way to the house. The Hermitage, an extravagant affair of gables and bay windows, is set back against the escarpment. A stand of Scots pine rears up dark green behind the house and bushland colours the extensive grounds olive green. Morning sun glints on several open casement windows. The house beckons, transfixed in time.

"However, did they build that staircase?" Vere asks.

"I'm not sure but let's test it shall we?" Roger stands back to let Vere go ahead, watching her swaying hips as she negotiates the stairs. John follows Roger, with the golden retriever at his heels. As they climb, the cry of a whipbird cracks the air and the dog barks in reply.

*

As soon as they set their luggage down in the hall, the men's hats on top, the grandfather clocks counts the hour of eleven. Roger is about to call out when a stout man in his early fifties puts his head around the nearest doorway and beckons them to join him.

"Welcome to the Hermitage. I'm Bernard Halliday." Bernard kisses Vere's hand quickly before she has a chance to withdraw it. He then shakes hands with both the men. "Pleased to meet Celeste's new guests. She won't be long. Come into the sitting room."

"Daphne," Bernard says, addressing the dog, "run along to Mrs Jenkins." The dog obliges by loping off towards the back of the house.

They are ushered into a pleasant room of dove grey walls and white standard lamps. Several chintz covered lounge chairs and two settees are assembled around a low table. Vere notices that Bernard was apparently reading an old illustrated journal that is now resting on the arm of his chair. She chooses a large lounge chair near their host's, leaving Roger and John to sit on the closest settee.

Roger asks after Mr Williams.

"Away at present. Rather nice to have male guests for a change. There's been a horde of women traipsing through lately." Bernard pauses and smiles at Vere. "Yourself excluded of course, my dear." Bernard points to a carved wooden box on the table. "Cigarette anyone? Cigar?"

"I'll have one. A cigarette, that is," Vere says. She gets up from her chair in a leisurely, fluid movement and takes one from the box.

"Allow me."

"Thanks," Vere says after Bernard has lit her cigarette with a heavy gold lighter. "Does Mrs. Williams entertain a lot?" She has moved towards the bay window to look at the view. Two small casement windows either side are open and Vere feels a light breeze on her face.

"Yes. It's a passion." Bernard pauses to exhale from his cigar. "She has an excellent cook housekeeper in Mrs. Jenkins

17

and she doesn't particularly like her own company. But not many of us do, do we?"

"No," Roger agrees.

"So, who are we and what do we do?"

"Vere Seymour-Smith and I'm a ticket writer at Buckley & Nunn."

"An artist in our midst."

"Hardly, although the view from this window is rather tempting."

"That's the Hermitage for you. Glorious views from nearly every window." Bernard blows a smoke ring and looks pointedly at the young man. "And you are?"

"John Summers, articled clerk."

"Well, well. We can talk shop later. I'm retired but still keep my hand in from time to time. Wills and Conveyancing." Bernard pauses to take a long puff from his cigar. "And you must be Roger?"

It is immediately obvious to Vere that Roger is slightly

annoyed at being spoken to last. She loves to people watch and is now quite prepared to have an entertaining time at the Hermitage.

"Yes, Maguire. Property development and I was wondering how we three came to be invited to the Hermitage. None of us can recall meeting Mr. and Mrs. Williams."

"Word of mouth, my dear boy. Celeste loves to entertain and here is the lady herself."

The three guests turn as Celeste Williams walks into the room. She is wearing a pale grey voile dress with a white collar and tiny white belt. Her hair curls around her face in soft waves and like Vere she is wearing bright red lipstick but unlike Vere it is startling against her pale complexion and her wheat-coloured hair. All three guests are stunned by her elegance and beauty. Only Vere detects something more and frowns.

"I'm so glad you could all come. I do hope you enjoy your stay. The Hermitage is such a soothing place. Ask Bernard. I can't get him to leave."

John and Vere laugh.

Bernard takes another long draw of his cigar. "Wait until you meet Blythe."

"I've just put her down, Bernard."

"You've always just put her down."

"Bernard darling, she's thirteen months old as you well know." Celeste pauses and smiles at her guest. "Blythe is my niece. I'm minding her while her parents are abroad."

"Abroad. Where?" Roger asks.

"At Menton."

Roger frowns. "On the French Riviera?

"Yes."

"I've always wanted to go," Roger says.

"It is beautiful. Particularly the gardens but I haven't been for years."

"How nice for them. And your husband is away I understand?"

Moving towards the table for another cigarette which

20

Bernard lights, Vere wonders why Roger is asking again. She notices a glance pass between Mrs. Williams and Bernard.

There is a swish of material as Celeste glides about the room. Slowly, she bends down to take a cigarette from the wooden box. This time John manages to light her cigarette before Roger, who is closest to her, has even begun to search for his lighter.

"Thank you," Celeste says, exhaling. "In London."

"On business?"

Suddenly Celeste takes a step backwards from the centre of the room. "I think lunch should be nearly ready. Excuse me whilst I go speak to Mrs. Jenkins."

Vere walks away from the window, circles the table and then settles herself on the arm of the settee closest to Roger. Bending close, she whispers in his ear. "Why are you being so rude?" She is sure no one else hears, yet Bernard cuts in.

"Celeste, although very hospitable is a private person. I would appreciate it if you respect her privacy, Mr. Maguire."

21

"I was only asking a few questions."

"It's your relentlessness, Roger," Vere says, blowing smoke out slowly towards the ceiling.

As Bernard considers what to say, Vere catches a tired expression on his face.

"Just a word to you all. A week at the Hermitage is something to be valued. But there are provisos." Bernard hesitates because Roger has now got up and begun pacing the room.

"Such as?" he asks.

"The obvious, Roger. And do sit down," Vere admonishes.

"Nothing stopping us from thrashing it out amongst ourselves. What do you say, John?" Roger asks, stopping in front of the younger man.

"I'm just glad to be here," John stammers in reply.

"Of course you are. And what about you, Vere? You don't want to know what all this is about? You had a few questions on the ferry if I recall."

"There is a time and place," Vere replies.

"Biding our time, are we?" Roger asks.

Vere gets up again and moves around the room, blowing smoke in Roger's direction as she passes him.

This action is not missed by Bernard. "Like to have everything clear cut and ship shape, Mr Maguire? In an ideal world, of course but unfortunately life isn't like that."

"Isn't it?" Roger replies, glaring at Vere. "I was just asking simple questions that only require simple answers."

"Really?" Vere asks, raising her eyebrows.

"Well, well, we mustn't get agitated. This is supposed to be a relaxing time for everyone. All will be revealed in good time. And now it seems lunch is ready. I can smell Mrs. Jenkins famous bacon and egg pie from here."

* * *

The Kitchen

The kitchen has been cleaned up after lunch and Mrs. Jenkins has left. Only Bernard and Celeste sit at the kitchen table. Both are smoking. Celeste is having a second cigarette – she generally only allows herself one a day - and Bernard, one of his ubiquitous cigars. They are also both sipping coffee.

Celeste rubs her forehead. "I thought we were dealing with three from September 1937. Instead, we've got two from 1937 and John from twenty years earlier. There must have been some sort of mix-up. I'm sure he wasn't due to arrive for another month."

"I think you're right and he's in a bad way. Very nervous and distracted. But with him being so bad, we might just get away with it."

Celeste finishes her coffee. "Well, just to be safe we can't mention the tennis court. He used to be a pretty good tennis player before the war evidently." Celeste pauses. "Maybe we

24

should do something about it?"

"What? Shroud the court like furniture?"

Celeste sighs. "You know what I mean, Bernard."

"What's the point? He'll find out eventually."

"True."

Bernard changes tack. "We do seem to have our hands full with Mr. Maguire."

"Yes. His intensity is very tiring. What happened to him?"

Bernard chuckles. "Stuck his neck out too far in his last business deal," he says, stubbing out his cigar.

Celeste almost chokes on her coffee. "And knowing your sense of humour Bernard, I'm guessing you mean that literally as well."

"Literally." Bernard chuckles.

Celeste is quick to reply. "I don't know how you can laugh about it. In light of your own circumstances."

"That was below the belt."

Celeste rubs her forehead again. "I know. I'm sorry. I'm

just so tired of it all."

Bernard takes both their coffee cups to the sink. "I know and I've told them."

"You have?"

"Yes, my dear. And this is the last group." Bernard stands behind her and puts his arms around her, crossing them at her waist.

They remain in companionable silence for a little while. Outside in the garden, near the pink and white azaleas, Roger can be heard reiterating some point, although the meaning isn't clear. After a moment Vere is heard saying: "You're not really making any sense, Roger." Then both can be heard walking away.

"I rather like Vere," Celeste says, shifting in her seat.

"So do I, but you'll have to be careful with her, C."

"How so?"

"She has an eye for detail. And I think she noticed your dress."

"My dress?" Celeste turns to face Bernard.

"Yes, that it wasn't quite right."

"Nonsense, Bernard. It is a perfectly suitable dress for lunch on a spring day."

Bernard removes his arms from Celeste. "Yes, but not for 1937."

"Really? I thought it would do."

"I'm afraid it was a wrong choice, my dear. You inadvertently jumped ahead a few years."

She sighs as Bernard moves away. "It's just a favourite of mine. I'll say something to cover it. Italy or some such. Or you can."

Celeste gets up and goes to the window overlooking the vegetable garden. The view seems to calm her and when she speaks again her tone is gentle. "It's John I'm worried about. I really don't know if I'm up to coping with his type of problem. I'm so glad they are our last group."

"We'll manage, darling. The ferry trip over is our only

other worry at the moment."

"How much he noticed on the way?"

"Precisely. And perhaps some quiet time with Blythe will help."

"No, I think Blythe is meant to work her magic on Roger."

"Really, C? What an interesting thought." They both push their chairs under the large oak table in unison.

"Shall we join your guests in the garden?" Bernard asks.

* * *

The Yew Tree Hedge

A lone magpie flies overhead, spying activity below. From a gum tree it observes the group of people disperse. Two wander off towards the left-hand side of the building near the kitchen and vegetable garden. The bird flies closer over the azaleas. There is a stone bench below a yew tree hedge that screens the vegetable garden from bushland. The two people sit down. Shadows loom below the yew tree and flicker across both their faces. The bird flies off towards the other side of the house, carolling as it goes.

"How are you, John?" Celeste asks.

"I'm very glad to be here, you know."

"I know you are. Not worried as to why you have been invited?"

"Just a little." He pauses. "I am worried about my clothes. I don't seem to be very presentable."

"Nonsense. You are very presentable but perhaps you

didn't bring enough with you?"

"Possibly not," John stammers.

"I can lend you a few shirts and trousers of my brother's. Would that help?"

"If...if you don't mind."

"Of course not."

Nervously, John begins to smooth the material of his trousers. "I haven't been well lately. I've had a lot of time off work."

"Have you? I'm sorry to hear that, John. Well, you definitely need a rest." Celeste pauses. "Now, I think Bernard mentioned some provisos. I have one as well."

John shifts awkwardly on the bench and Celeste touches his hand to still his movement.

"What is it?" he asks.

She smiles gently at him. "To not dwell too much on the past. Just enjoy where you are now and this lovely spring day."

"It is a beautiful day."

They sit for a few moments in silence. "I want you to rest and relax and everything will become clear."

John frowns but again the touch of Celeste's hand calms him. "We have a good library here and beautiful grounds as you can see." Celeste stands up with a soft whispering sound, the pale grey of her dress, glowing in the dim light. "Just enjoy your stay here."

"I'll try to." John watches in awe as Celeste moves off.

"Don't forget the library," Celeste calls as she nears the kitchen door.

"I..I... won't." John gets up and walks away from the hedge. He looks about him at the olive green bushland catching the afternoon light and then back at the house. He doesn't remember seeing anything so welcoming in all his life.

* * *

On the terrace

In the brief moment before Bernard joins the remaining two guests on the terrace, he can't help smiling at the orchestration of wispy clouds, a gentle breeze in the gum trees and the warbling of magpies. As he nears the terrace, he decides that the hydrangeas beginning to bloom are a nice touch.

Bernard notices a lone magpie sitting on the stump of an old pine tree that had to be cut back years ago. The bird cocks his head at Bernard. A spy? Bernard wonders. On reconnaissance? He laughs at the absurd thought but then anything is possible in this place. As he takes his seat, there is the sound of clinking class.

Mrs Jenkins places a tray of home-made lemonade on the table and bustles away.

"Thank you, Mrs Jenkins. Who's for a glass of lemonade?"

Roger ignores the question. "Now that we've got you

alone, Bernard, are you going to tell us why we are really here?"

Vere takes a glass of lemonade. "Will you let it go, Roger. It seems none of us are meant to be anywhere else. At least I don't think I should be."

"No, I won't let it go! And I should be somewhere else. I'm in the middle of a very big business deal and perhaps you want in. Is that why I'm here?" Roger directs the last question at Bernard.

"Your North Shore purchase?"

Roger jumps to his feet, pushing back his chair which falls awkwardly to the ground. "What the hell!"

"Don't worry, dear boy. I don't have any intention of purchasing land north of here. I'll stay where I am, close to the harbour."

Roger rights his chair and begins pacing. He wonders briefly why he is always pacing in such a peaceful place but then dismisses the thought. "How did you hear about it?"

"Conveyancing, dear boy. I still keep my hand in and I

have a wide circle of acquaintances."

"So, you think it's too far from the city as well, do you?"

"I didn't say that," Bernard remarks, a slight annoyance in his tone.

"It's just bush, Roger. No trams or buses. I would need a car to get to work and that's just not in my budget."

"Yes, but as I said earlier, Vere, you are not a potential buyer anyway. This is beyond your pocketbook."

Vere glares at him. "Why are we talking about your business deal now, Roger? It sounds like you need a rest from the project."

"Here, here," Bernard says, studying both of them. "Why don't you indulge me Roger, in an experiment. I want you to pretend it's all over. Your business deal, that is. All the blocks have been sold and you've made your money. You are now having a week off."

"Easier said than done."

"Try," Bernard says as he lights a cigarette for Vere.

34

"Thanks."

"I insist," Bernard says.

"Fine."

As Roger sits down again there is a chorus of approval from the magpies in the gum trees.

"I know they have dreadful nesting habits but you can't help love their song."

"Yes, quite right, Vere. We have a lot of birds around the Hermitage. Now Roger," Bernard turns his genial host face towards the recalcitrant younger man. "Tell me your plans for this evening and tomorrow."

"What time is it?" Roger asks.

Vere glances at her wristwatch. "It's 5 o'clock."

"I'll read the papers before dinner."

"We don't keep the papers here."

"What? You must be joking. And why are you looking like that, Vere. Like you are in on a joke?"

"I'm just not surprised, that's all."

35

Bernard sips his lemonade. "It's Celeste's wish. She can't stand all the news from Europe. It upsets her."

"That Chancellor fellow?"

"Yes," Bernard replies.

"He's got nothing to do with us," Roger says.

"Quite. But she has her quirks, our Celeste."

"And beautiful clothes. Like the dress she is wearing today."

Bernard looks away briefly. "I believe she got that dress from Rome. She has a cousin who married a local and she sends her the odd dress from time to time."

"Rome. Oh, how wonderful. I would love to go!"

"Think of the sketching you could do." Bernard stands up and pushes his chair back. "Now, Roger. The Hermitage has quite a decent library. All the classics. Stendhal, Sir Walter Scott, Thackeray. Celeste likes short story collections. She has O. Henry and H.G. Wells. I recommend both."

Roger puffs out his cheeks in annoyance. "You can hunt

me out the O. Henry."

"Done. And what about you, Vere?"

"Any good murder mystery will do."

"We'll check the shelves together. And how about some sketching tomorrow?

"I didn't bring any supplies with me," Vere says, getting up also.

"Will a sketch pad and pencils do?"

"At a pinch. But a few 2 and 4Bs would be lovely and maybe some charcoal."

"I think we might be in luck."

"Really?" Vere asks, raising her eyebrows.

"A previous guest was a rather good artist."

"Oh, I am lucky then. Who was it? I go to as many exhibitions as I can."

Bernard bends down to put the empty glasses back on the tray. "Obscure but good." Bernard straightens up. "I'll just take these back to Mrs Jenkins."

"He left his supplies behind?" Roger asks.

Bernard cuts in quickly. "Any hobbies Roger?"

Roger frowns at Bernard and takes his time answering. "No."

"Walking?"

"Never much seen the point of walking."

"That doesn't surprise me," Vere says.

"And what do you mean by that?"

Vere pushes her chair in. "That you are not relaxed enough to enjoy a good walk. You would want to gain something from it other than the walk itself."

"And what am I supposed to say to that?"

"Nothing. Just prove me wrong perhaps." She moves off with Bernard to the house, leaving Roger alone with his thoughts.

* * *

Blythe's Bedroom

The wind has caught the child's mobile. It tinkles as the child wakes.

"My darling, you are awake. And we have new guests. There is one I especially want you to meet."

Celeste turns swiftly at the sound of footsteps behind her. "And here he is the man himself. I didn't expect you in the baby's room but now you're here, Roger, this is Blythe."

"That's what I get for nosing around."

Celeste picks the baby up and walks towards Roger who is looking tense. As Celeste moves closer to Roger the baby stretches out her hands and almost touches Roger's cheek.

She is the most beautiful child he has ever seen and without thinking he takes the child's small hand. "Pleased to meet you, Blythe. Although I prefer the company of people who can talk."

Celeste smiles and hugs the child. "Oh, Blythe can talk.

Just not in the ordinary sense."

"Meaning?"

"She senses people's moods and she's very restful to be around. Maybe by the end of the week we'll have you enjoying her company."

Roger looks sceptical. "She will be eating with us, will she?"

"The occasional meal. I'm afraid she is still a little messy with her food. Sometimes I like to bring her into the sitting room of an evening. She crawls around and generally spends time with each of the guests."

"And is this part of the rest cure of the Hermitage? Learning to enjoy an infant's company?"

"I wouldn't rule it out."

Celeste smiles sweetly at Roger and walks off, leaving him standing in the doorway. He appears disconcerted and looks around the baby's room as if for answers to everything that is troubling him. As Celeste walks down the hall, the baby looks back in his direction.

* * *

THE SECOND DAY

Vere's bedroom

Moonlight is streaming through Vere's guest room shining on
the alarm clock on her bedside table showing 3.10 a.m. and also
highlighting Vere's belongings that are scattered about the room.
She has obviously been through her suitcase looking for
something and she is now pacing about in a distracted manner.
Stubbing out her cigarette Vere leaves her room, walking out on
to the terrace by a French window. She is wearing only a thin
negligee.

* * *

Celeste's bedroom

Celeste and Bernard are in bed together. Bernard turns over towards Celeste. "What time is it?"

"It's nearly 3.30."

"God awful hour. How long has Vere been awake?"

"All night."

"You'd better go. She'll be out on the terrace by now."

"Yes, I'd better," Celeste says, sitting up.

"Don't forget your dressing gown."

"It's here on the end of the bed." Celeste puts her sleeves into an elegant white silk wrap and shrugs it on.

"And take a dressing gown with you for Vere. She won't have put one on."

Celeste is not surprised by Bernard's remark. She simply replies, "Quite."

*

On the terrace moments later there is the sound of a frog croaking and someone walking up and down.

"Celeste?" Vere asks the dark night.

"Yes," Celeste answers softly. "I'm here. Can you see me? I have a wrap for you." Vere moves towards the sound of Celeste's voice. The older woman folds a pale blue dressing gown around Vere's shoulders. "Come and sit down." Celeste gestures to the white table and chairs nearby, glowing suddenly as the moonlight falls on them.

"Oh, the moon's back," Vere says, looking about her in a confused state.

"Sit down, Vere," Celeste repeats.

Vere obeys, gathering her flowing negligee about her legs and wrapping the dressing gown around her, all the while trying to collect her thoughts. "I've got myself into an awful state. I can't remember organising the week off work."

"I sent the cards out a month ago. I'm sure you would

44

have, Vere."

"Then I must have but I can't remember speaking to Mr. Hodges about it. He can be an awful bastard and I'm sure he would have had a thing or two to say. Some self-righteous remark about uppity young ladies who think they are irreplaceable." Vere pauses. "He barely gives me any ticket writing to do. Mainly dressing store dummies." Vere glances at Celeste. "It must seem stupid to you. My job."

"Not at all. It's a job of course but it incorporates your art."

"My art. It's hardly that. Just sketching." Vere moves in her seat.

"Nevertheless, you are here and therefore it must be all right, don't you think?"

"Obviously," Vere says sighing, "but it worries me I can't remember. And, I have this nagging feeling I've forgotten something." Vere turns towards the French windows of her room where her beside lamp shines in a small halo. Her suitcase is flung open like a gaping mouth and her clothes are everywhere. "As you can see, I've made a right mess looking for God knows what."

"We don't need to worry about that now."

"I am so sorry! Was it me that woke you? I didn't think but then I can be very selfish as my mother likes to point out."

"Well, she's not here now."

"Thank God!"

Celeste laughs softly. "Surely she's not that bad."

"She's the reason why I don't get up before 11 o'clock on the weekends. Every chance she gets she criticises me. She never got over my father's death when I was a child."

"I'm sorry to hear that. As I said she's not here now. Why don't you sleep in tomorrow? We can have breakfast without you."

"That would be lovely. But what about the thing I have forgotten?"

"I expect it will come to you."

"Thank you, Celeste. You truly are the perfect hostess."

Vere kisses Celeste quickly on the cheek and is about to leave when Celeste speaks.

"The men will miss you though."

"Too bad. I'm sure I will catch up with them later."

"Particularly John."

Vere moves towards her room but slows at Celeste's last remark, her hand on the door frame of the French windows. As she turns towards Celeste, she notices the moonlight has fallen on the older woman, blurring the outline of her body to a soft glow. She is almost incandescent. Vere rubs her eyes at the vision and shakes her head. "He's just a boy and he's not what I'm looking for."

"Don't be too sure," the vision says.

"I'm sure." Vere moves quickly back inside not giving Celeste a chance to reply.

Celeste smiles and whispers to herself, "He's older than he looks."

Morning

Suddenly the house erupts in sound. Blythe is crying, Daphne is barking, doors open and close quickly. Footsteps can be heard and then the baby stops crying abruptly when someone picks her up.

Roger is shouting. "You didn't go on the bloody walk that I've been on so don't try and tell me I'm being unreasonable!"

"I'm so...sorry. I don't understand."

"What do you understand, John?" Roger asks in a nasty tone.

Celeste enters the hall with Blythe on her hip. Roger is clearly surprised to see the baby and is disconcerted by the child's quiet contemplation of him. He falls silent.

"Breakfast everyone? Vere won't be joining us," Celeste says.

*

Order has been reinstated with a severe warning from Bernard.
Breakfast is now underway. Tea is being sipped. Toast buttered
and cups clinking but the reprieve is brief.

Roger puts down his teacup with a clatter. "I want to know
what the hell is going on."

"I don't exactly know what the problem is, old boy."

"Don't old boy me. You know perfectly well what the
matter is." Roger pauses for effect. "We are all prisoners here!"

John chokes on his tea while Celeste sighs and offers
another piece of toast to Blythe. She watches as the baby takes it
from her hand. "So, you didn't enjoy your walk?"

"I've been walking for over two hours!"

"That was a bit extreme," Bernard says, waving a piece of
toast in the air. "I was merely advocating a stroll yesterday."

"A stroll. It wasn't a stroll. It was like no walk I've ever
been on. I couldn't escape this bloody place. Just kept going
round and round in fucking circles!"

"I'll have none of that!" Bernard slams his fist down on the table making the teacups rattle again.

Blythe widens her eyes but doesn't cry and Celeste sips her tea with her head bowed.

"There'll be no swearing in the Hermitage. None of it, do you hear!"

"None of this. None of that." Roger is muttering now. "Yes, I'll have no more of that, I can tell you. I won't be going on another walk in a hurry. Every path leads back here. No matter which way I went."

"Wh... what do you mean? Roger."

Roger makes a concerted effort to calm his thoughts. "I thought I'd head towards Cremorne Road. I cut back behind the Hermitage. Everything was familiar. Green Street was in sight when suddenly I was surrounded by bush again. Bush and nothing else. I couldn't believe it. I was actually on a walking trail behind the house. I started again. This time I walked along the bay heading for Rialto Avenue. Thought I'd at least try and make MacCallum Pool but no such luck. Before I knew it I was staring at the bloody Scots Pines at the back of this blasted place." Roger waves towards the back of the Hermitage.

"The rock pool?" John asks.

Roger shakes his head, ignoring the younger man. "So, do you want to tell me what is going on, Bernard? Are we prisoners here?"

"And how, exactly are we keeping you here?" Bernard begins buttering another slice of toast, making Roger wait as he applies marmalade. He looks up and adds, "By supernatural forces?"

John is concentrating on his porridge. Celeste is quietly sipping her tea. Blythe coos and giggles.

Roger looks askance at the baby. "Why can't I leave this God-forsaken place?"

"You can leave anytime as long as one of us accompanies you."

"What! So, you both have magical powers, do you?"

John coughs into his porridge.

"I will leave, when I damn well choose to leave. And where's Vere?"

"She asked not to be disturbed. She had trouble sleeping last night," Celeste says calmly.

"I'll recommend a bracing walk to her this afternoon and let's see how far she gets."

* * *

THE THIRD DAY

In the Garden

It is the afternoon of the following day. The gum trees on the highest point of the Hermitage stand sentinel, towering above the pine trees. They are swaying in a wind that is almost singing in the bright sunshine. John and Vere sit breathless on the stone bench below the yew tree hedge. They are both exhausted.

Vere wipes sweat from her forehead. "So, it seems, Roger was right." She stops for breath. "We can't leave here." Vere pauses again. "I had a sneaking suspicion we mightn't be able to but didn't want to give Roger the satisfaction of being right yesterday."

John is still struggling to breathe. "He'll find out today."

"Yes. I expect he's waiting in the sitting room, ready to gloat."

John looks around him at the vegetable garden and the

gum trees waving their branches overhead. "Could we have missed a turning? I mean a lot of the bay looks different from what I remember."

"In what way?"

"More blocks of flats. Less trees, except for here." He seems mesmerised by the gum trees and the pines. "For instance, I don't remember that large square block of flats near the point," John says, frowning.

"Montana?"

"Is that what they are called?"

"You don't remember the Montana flats?" Vere is studying him carefully now. "Have you been away?"

No, but perhaps I just haven't walked right down to the wharf. I can't remember the last time I did in fact."

"Cremorne Wharf?"

"Yes. Were we close?" John asks, pulling at his collar and pushing his hair out of his eyes.

"Deceptively," Vere says faintly. In a happier tone she

remarks, "Well at least we've found out there's a tennis court."

"Yes. But perhaps they don't want us to use the court?"

"Why ever not?"

"Well, they never mentioned it."

"No, but they can't think of everything. I mean they have been the perfect hosts."

"They have been. So much so I don't mind that we can't leave for the moment."

"You don't?" Vere asks.

"No. And I don...don't think you do either."

"How perceptive of you." Vere lights a cigarette. Why don't you mind?"

"I don't seem to have anywhere else to go."

"Really?"

John is clearly becoming more nervous. He stands up and begins to walk up and down. As he passes Vere for the second or third time, she grabs his hand. He stares down at her and she smiles up at him sympathetically. There is a crash of pots and pans from the kitchen which makes them both smile.

"It's fine. You can tell me."

There is a long moment as they exchange glances. Finally, John sits back down next to Vere.

"After I left home, I was living for a while in Raglan Street with my friends, two chaps." John pushes his hair off his forehead again. "I met them a while ago but now I've lost touch with them."

"Where were you living when you got the invitation?" Vere asks, blowing smoke out slowly above her head. She watches as John becomes more agitated.

"You see, that's the thing. I can't remember. I think I must have just found it in my pocket."

"Funny you should say that. I can't remember where I was either when I got my invitation. I thought I was at my mother's house in Sydney but I somehow organised a week off work for my job in Melbourne but I don't remember phoning my boss."

"You must have."

56

"Yes, I must have."

"I think I've been ill. That's why I've forgotten so much. I tried to find my parent's house a while ago and I was sure I had the correct address."

"Where?"

"In Spofforth Street. But there was a corner shop in place of the house. It was the right place because the camphor laurel was still out the back but someone had converted the front of the house into a shop front. My parents would never do that, so I must be remembering wrong."

"But what about the camphor laurel?"

"Maybe I was mixed up about that. I get so confused these days."

Vere places her hand briefly over John's. "It's all right."

"I even tried to find my place of work. They were in Elizabeth Street, number 140. And I'm very sure about that." John rubs his forehead. "Well, I was there the other day and they seem to have moved too. How can that be?"

"So, you don't work there now?"

"Vere, I don't know."

They exchange glances again and this time Vere takes in his light brown hair, green eyes and neat features. He really is good looking, she realises. "I think I can help."

"I'm going mad."

"Well then, I am too."

John is stammering again. "No, you are not."

"Are you arguing with me now?"

John is shocked at Vere's question and as a result she bursts out laughing. "I don't bite, you know. Let's see if we can work this all out. How about I get Mrs. Jenkins to make us some tea and we can go over everything together?"

"Th... that would be nice."

*

A little while later Vere is alone in the library, carefully examining the shelves on both sides of the room. She stands still for a moment thinking and then quickly pulls out a book on one of the lower shelves. She holds it close to her body, in the folds of her skirt, as she makes her way back to her room.

* * *

The Sitting Room

The grandfather clock in the hall chimes the hour of five and
Bernard is rustling the pages of one of his old, illustrated
journals. Celeste is reading a book which she puts down to study
Bernard.

"Bernard, I've got to see to Blythe. Can you remove the
street directory and the touring map from the library? I think
Vere will be looking for both soon."

"What makes you say that?"

"Just an inkling. And I don't want her to locate either of
them. It's only the third day. And it will be too much for John.
Sydney will be unrecognisable to him."

"I think she's ready."

"But John isn't," Celeste argues.

"You're quite adamant about this, aren't you? I've never
seen you so protective before."

"You know why, Bernard. He's one of our special ones

and if we are going to be honest with each other then, frankly,
I'm surprised that you aren't spending more time with him.
There was talk on the first day of discussing law, all chummy."
Celeste stresses the last word. "And since then you've avoided
him like the plague. I thought you would want to spend time
with him. After all, didn't he..."

Bernard cuts in angrily. "I don't want to talk about it. How
often have I forbidden it?"

"Yes, you have but now that I'm leaving soon, I think you
should be the one that speaks to John and explains what has
happened to him." Celeste sighs deeply. "When you do, I will be
here to help. And it might be good for you to talk about Byron."

"I don't want to talk about my son! And I don't want to
talk to John. Let Vere deal with him." Bernard raises his voice
another notch. "Byron's gone and that's the end of it!"

Celeste is laughing, almost uncontrollably. "Oh Bernard.
For us that's always the beginning. As you well know." She
covers her mouth with her hand for a moment and attempts to

recover her composure. Bernard ignores her by picking up another journal to read. After a moment she stands up and begins walking around the room. "So, what shall we do about the Gregory's and the map?"

"I will hide them in my room for now. We've got the storm to cope with tonight."

Celeste stops walking. "It's not tonight, is it? Maybe he won't wake up."

"Oh, he will."

"Nothing happened to him with the ruckus Roger caused the first morning."

"Quite obviously Roger yelling and stomping around."

"Oh, I don't know." Celeste sighs. "Is he still bothered by it all?" Celeste stops by Bernard's chair and looks down at him. "I mean, does he remember enough to be bothered?"

Bernard closes his paper with a loud rustle. "We shall soon find out."

"Well, I don't think Vere is ready if he does start tonight

and what are we to do about Roger? We don't want him waking up and wandering about."

"I'll take care of Roger. Please just take care of the other two, C." He takes Celeste's hand and looks up at her with deep affection.

The door opens and closes and Roger is in front of them. "Well, well, isn't this a picture of marital bliss? Except, of course, Mr Williams is absent."

"Oh, have you been for a walk again, Roger?" Celeste asks.

"Yes, and with the same results."

"How about a walk this evening?"

"Is that meant to be a joke, Bernard?"

"On the contrary. I know a delightful watering hole not far from here."

"Are we all going?"

"No, just the two of us. You can tell me about your North Shore development."

"Is this some kind of trick?"

"A walk to the pub? Hardly."

Celeste stands up. "Would you rather stay in, Roger?"

"No, I bloody well wouldn't. But why aren't the other two invited?"

"John doesn't drink and Vere..."

Roger cuts in. "Yes, I know. I'm not her favourite person. She has said as much."

Bernard and Celeste exchange a quick glance, a smile just grazing Celeste's lips.

"Around 7.30 then?" Bernard asks.

"Wouldn't it be pretty dark by then?" Roger asks in a mock tone. "I mean we wouldn't want to get lost."

"Don't worry. I know my way."

"That's settled then." Celeste moves towards the door of the sitting room.

"You have no excuse now Celeste not to finish the Virginia Woolf you've been reading for years."

"It's The Years, Bernard." Celeste smiles as at the antics of a small child. Bernard winks mischievously at Celeste, unseen by Roger. He is busy searching his pocket for a cigarette.

After finding a cigarette Roger asks, "And what are Vere's plans?"

"Oh, I think she's reading too."

Roger narrows his eyes at both of them, only now aware that he has missed something. He gazes at his cigarette in his right hand and walks out of the room, patting his pockets with his left hand for his lighter.

*

Vere is in Celeste's room. She glances nervously about her and looks at two books on Celeste's bedside table, inspecting the inside flaps of both books.

*

In Blythe's bedroom a small lamp with giraffes around the edge is on and the room is bathed in a soft glow. Celeste bends over the baby.

"Now you know not to wake, don't you, darling?"

The baby smiles and reaches up towards Celeste. Celeste holds the small hand in hers for a moment, kisses the baby and then leaves the room.

* * *

The Library

Celeste is alone in the room plumping up cushions on the window seat. She looks about the room and turns off the main overhead light. After a moment she turns on the other standard lamp. Both shine out softly illuminating the bookshelves on either side of the room. As it is a small room there is only a two-seater couch facing the window seat, built into the bay window and no other chairs.

The bay windows are aglow with glinting lights from the harbour. A ferry, ablaze with lights, can be seen making slow progress across the water towards the left. With an abrupt movement Celeste draws the curtains and then turning slowly, checks the peanuts and small hors de oeuvres on the low table. As she is about to leave, the dog pads in, swinging its tail.

"Can't find John, Daphne?"

The dog sits up keenly and wags its tail again.

"You have been shadowing him, haven't you? But it's

time to go to bed." Celeste is about to take the dog's collar in her hand when she stops and stands up. "Perhaps not," she says to herself. "But you must be good." She bends down and pats the soft coat of the golden retriever.

Daphne wags her tail even faster. "Keep away from the food and don't get under their feet."

*

Daphne barks as John and Vere enter the library.

"Well hello, Daphne. What are you doing in here?"

"Daphne. I had forgotten that was her name. I wonder if she named her after the writer. Celeste seems to be such a reader."

"Is there a writer named Daphne? I haven't heard of her."

Vere is about to say something then changes her mind. "You probably read mainly men. I find most men do. I want to read her book Jamaica Inn. It sounds fascinating. I'm hoping I can borrow it whilst I'm here."

John doesn't appear to have heard her. "Do you mind if Daphne stays here?"

"I don't mind at all," Vere replies, watching John's smiling face as he pats the dog.

Vere moves the bowls of food to an empty part of the bookshelf on the left of the room and softly closes the door to the hall. "I think this is a nicer room than the sitting room."

"Yes, I think it is."

As Vere begins to check the shelves, John sits back in the couch with the dog at his feet. "Now I wonder if they have a street directory." Vere searches most of the shelves in earnest. "No luck." She stops for a moment and then pulls out two books. "Now this is a silly question but what do you think of time travel, John? Do you believe it's possible?"

"Like H.G. Wells, The Time Machine?"

"Yes."

"I've heard about it but haven't read it. I prefer books set in Australia. Stories about the bush mostly."

"How about Jonah by Louis Stone?" Vere moves the book in her right hand, indicating it is the one she is holding.

"I read that a couple of years ago."

Vere checks the date and something is confirmed in her mind. "Did you? Do you know it was published in 1911? That's 26 years ago"

"I don't understand. What do you mean?"

Vere sits down next to John on the couch. Keeping her voice calm Vere asks, "Have you read this one?" She passes John the other book. "I'm sure you would have enjoyed it. It's a book about animals and it's set in the Queensland Hills."

John takes the book carefully and looks at the cover. "Man-Shy. Sounds like my kind of book but I don't think I've heard of this one. I might read it while we're here."

"Have a look at the date of publication," Vere says gently.

John finds the end papers and the date of publication.

"Does it look strange to you? The date?"

John is clearly confused. He glances awkwardly from Vere's face to the book and back again. "It does a bit."

Vere moves to the shelves and picks up two more books which she places at her feet. John has turned away to pat the dog.

"I'm going to ask you some more questions about books. Is that okay?"

John nods, unable to speak.

"Good." Vere studies John. "Now, I love puzzles, so I tend to read a lot of detective novels. Have you heard of Agatha Christie?" Vere hands him one of the two books from the floor.

John glances at the front cover but is still unable to speak.

"This is her first book. The Mysterious Affair at Styles. Have a look at the date."

"1920."

Vere hands him the second book. "Here's another of hers. "The Murder of Roger Ackroyd."

John looks for the date without Vere asking. "1926. Is she a famous writer?"

"Yes. A very famous mystery writer. Have you heard of her?"

"No."

"Perhaps you don't like lady writers."

John bites his lip. "Maybe I should have heard of her."

"How about John Dickson Carr? He writes locked room mysteries. And we seem to be locked up here, don't we?" Vere sighs in frustration. She hates feeling nervous. She takes a cigarette from the pocket of her dress and lights it from the heavy silver lighter on the table.

"I haven't heard of him or a locked room mystery."

"Oh, John." Vere frowns in dismay. "How about the mystery of the Hermitage?"

"Is that what we are trying to solve?"

"Yes." Vere sits back down on the couch and touches John's cheek. It's September 1937. What year do you think it is?" Vere hesitates. I don't mean to frighten you."

"It can't be! That doesn't sound right. It just can't be."

"It is. You are missing about twenty years. Your clothes for instance. The ones you brought with you."

"My clothes. Are they all wrong?"

Vere nods in reply.

"What's the matter with me? Why can't I remember?"

"It's not just you, John. It's the three of us, although Roger is no help at all." Vere straightens her back, thinking. "I know for a fact it is 1937. I believe it is still 1937 but I think I'm missing a few weeks."

"But you're saying I've lost twenty years. Do you think I've travelled forward somehow and don't realise it?"

"Yes. Somehow. You can remember a book published in 1911 but nothing after it. Am I right?"

"It seems so. Not that I read that much. But how is that possible? Is that why they don't have any papers here so we can't check the date."

"Maybe. Or part of the whole thing. The whole locked room thing. I haven't worked it out yet." Vere gets up and begins to pace the room while smoking her cigarette. "Earlier this evening I snuck into Celeste's room and found something very interesting."

"What?"

"A book called The Pursuit of Love published in 1945."

"1945? Do you think it's 1945 now?"

"No, I still think it is 1937. This house breathes 1937. But not Bernard and Celeste. I think they are time travellers. The 1945 book and the dress Celeste wore the first day we arrived." Vere stops in front of John.

"She's very beautiful."

"Yes, she is. But there is something sad about her, don't you think?"

"Maybe," John says.

"And what about the baby? Where is the mother? And where's Celeste's husband?"

John rubs his eyes. Vere places a hand on his shoulder. "You don't have to answer all these questions. I'm just thinking aloud."

Vere begins pacing again while her cigarette burns low. Eventually, she stubs it out in the ashtray on the low table. As she straightens up, she narrows her eyes at a title on the bookshelf to the left of the room. She moves quickly and retrieves the book. It is the 1936 Gregory's. "Oh, here it is!" Vere flips through the pages until she finds Mosman. She hands the book to John.

He looks at the directory. "That's not Mosman. There's too many streets." He hesitates. "Where's the bush gone?"

"Twenty years has taken the bush, John. More housing and new roads."

"No. That's not right." John puts his head in his hands.

Vere pats him gently, running her hands tenderly across the top of his head as she walks past him. "I've been meaning to make myself a drink for the last twenty minutes. I'm having a whisky. What would you like?"

"I'm sorry, Vere. I don't drink."

"I think you need to make an exception for tonight. I'll make you a brandy." Vere moves towards a small drinks trolley in the right-hand corner of the room. She mixes her whisky with ice and pours John's brandy, walking past the right-hand bookshelf before sitting back down with John. At the last moment something catches her eye. Quickly and spilling some of the liquid, Vere puts the drinks down and moves swiftly to the second last shelf. With an excited movement, Vere retrieves a touring map and opens it.

"A 1910 touring map!" Vere scans the map and locates Mosman. "Your Mosman, John?"

John studies the map for a moment and then lets it drop to the floor. He again cradles his head in his hands and begins to rock forward slightly in his seat. Vere watches him for a moment and then finally kneels down and takes his head in her hands. His face is streaked from crying. She kisses him passionately and Vere is caught off guard when he returns her kiss with equal passion. After a little while, Vere pulls away and whispers something in John's ear as she stands up.

"Your room?"

"Yes, tonight. Soon. But have your drink first and I'll have mine."

Vere watches the young man closely as he nervously sips his brandy, Daphne lying at his feet.

* * *

Away

Bernard and Roger arrive at a large hotel ablaze with lights and with people standing outside on the balcony. Talk and laughter drift down. Roger notices the name spelt out in large letters under the eaves: The Wycombe Hotel. Both men stop and look up at the drinkers on the balcony. The front door is open and the lighted interior beckons. Bernard appears ready to stride inside but Roger has halted and is looking around him.

"Why haven't I heard of this place?"

"Small private hotel with select clientele, Roger."

At that moment a young woman leans perilously over the railing of the balcony and yells out, "Teddy, darling, I'm sorry. I didn't mean it."

Both men turn automatically looking for Teddy, but he is nowhere in sight.

"Select clientele, indeed! Don't play games with me, Bernard!"

"Who, me?"

Roger is about to answer when a young woman wearing a beaded dress flounces out the front door followed by a young man in white flannels.

"What's this? A flapper party?" Roger asks in a sarcastic tone.

"More likely fancy dress, old boy." Not waiting for Roger, Bernard walks inside. Roger reluctantly follows. The two men find the place is abuzz but manage to secure their drinks without too much delay and, after a moment, a table on the balcony.

"Well, this is perfect! See where you can end up when you go for a walk."

Roger glances with annoyance at Bernard, blows air out of his cheeks and takes a sip of his beer. "Anyone here you know?"

Bernard has moved to stand at the balcony. He looks about him at the dark bay, the soft lights of houses and the full moon shining down. "Isn't this a wonderful night? Quite warm for spring, don't you think?"

"Look, there's something odd about this place," Roger says, staring at the people sitting at a nearby table.

"Odd? In what way?"

"Well, their clothes for one thing. Their heartiness for another."

"Not everyone is as world weary as you, Roger. You've been trudging too long down the halls of commerce and double dealing, dear boy."

Roger glances swiftly at Bernard but decides to ignore his last remark. He is suddenly sick of arguing. He takes a deep breath. "Maybe I have."

Bernard reaches for Roger's empty glass. "Now why don't I get you another drink?"

"I don't mind if you do," Roger says, forcing himself to be cheerful. Several beers later Roger discovers he does feel quite cheerful after all.

*

The moon, all seeing, cuts a swathe of pearly light from Bradleys Head, to the zoo, sweeping west to Sirius Cove, Mosman, to Cremorne, Kurraba Point and Kirribilli and then back to Cremorne. The beam hones in on white railings and a mooring light out on the bay. Nearby are two figures weaving their way down a path leading to the Hermitage. After a moment the beam shifts until it falls on two people naked on a bed.

Vere notices the moonlight grazing half of the bed. It is like a blessing, almost empowering. John is hesitant that much is obvious; slowly Vere takes charge.

*

By the time the storm crashes in the sky, Bernard and Roger are home - Bernard in Celeste's arms, Roger in his own room snoring loudly.

Storm

The sound of steady rain falling and Roger snoring is split by a crack of thunder. Immediately a man screams and Celeste closes her eyes in distress. How is she going to get through this? She can't do it alone. There is another clap of thunder.

"Bernard, wake up! It's started."

Bernard sits up quickly and is out of bed in an instant. Celeste struggles to move upright. She watches as he throws a dressing gown on and heads into the hall to lock Roger's door.

"You'll need to go to them soon," Bernard says when he returns.

"I'm not ready yet."

*

In Vere's room John has scrambled from the bed and is now crouched beside it, cowering. He yells, "Get down, get down!"

Vere's sits huddled on the bed, bewildered, as she looks down at John on the floor.

"They're firing on us. Meadows's been hit. Get down! Get down! They're coming for us. Get down!"

"John, John. Please stop. Whatever is the matter?"

John lowers his voice. "They're not going to keep marching us. Did you hear me?" he asks, looking up in Vere's direction. "They're not going to keep marching us."

Vere is crying now. "Stop it, John. Stop it. Please come back to bed."

"No! No. You don't understand." John stands up suddenly, frightening Vere.

"Please stop John. Please."

At that moment Celeste knocks on Vere's door. Slowly Vere opens it. Behind both woman, John frantically paces around the bed. The bedside light from Celeste's bedroom throws a meagre light in the room but it is enough to highlight the fear in both women's faces. For a moment neither woman speaks. When the exhausted Vere hops back on to the bed and rests her head on her knees, Celeste moves towards the pacing John. He narrowly misses knocking into her twice but when she finally manages to put her hands on his shoulders, he stops suddenly. "John, you're here with us. With me. With Vere. No-one can hurt you now."

John remains still but there is a vacant expression on his face.

"What's the matter with him? What's he talking about?" Vere asks.

Celeste ignores the questions. "John, you're at the Hermitage."

He notices Celeste first and then Vere. "Christ, my head hurts!" Bending down, he puts his head in his hands and begins to cry.

Vere rushes to his side.

"I'll leave you with him. The worst is over."

Celeste tiptoes back to her room, opening and closing the door softly. The mantle clock on Celeste's bureau chimes midnight as she gets into bed.

"What did you say to Vere?"

"What could I say?"

"I'll try the Spanish Civil War on them tomorrow at breakfast."

"That's not going to work, Bernard but I suppose it's worth a try. At least we didn't have to deal with Roger."

"Yes, I made sure he had a lot to drink."

"You didn't take him to the Wycombe, did you?"

"Yes I did but it was fine. The visit lulled him into a false sense of security. But I believe a tennis match will be proposed tomorrow."

"Oh dear. Then we'd better try and get some sleep." After a moment Celeste turns back towards Bernard. "You did remove

85

the Gregory's and the map like I asked, didn't you?"

"No, I decided not to. We can't keep delaying the inevitable."

"Oh Bernard." Celeste sighs. She switches off the bedside lamp.

"They have to work through these things, C."

"Like the tennis match?" Celeste asks, closing her eyes.

"Yes, like the tennis match," Bernard replies softly.

*

An hour later the sky is clear as if there never was a storm. The moon is back shining on the terrace and grazing the foot of Vere's bed and moving towards the door. She sits up contemplating the moonlight and the sleeping form of her lover. With a frustrated movement she hops out of bed and picks up John's discarded white shirt. She examines the collar carefully and then throws it aside.

THE FOURTH DAY

The Tennis Court

Vere is sitting with John on a bench near the court watching
Roger and Celeste play tennis. For most of the game Roger has
been stalking his end of the court like a tiger and having trouble
with his serve. Although Roger is playing erratically, Celeste
manages to return every ball with elegance and precision.

A large gum tree throws shadows across the court and
keeps Vere and John out of the sun. As the game progresses the
players move in and out of the shade.

As the second game begins John asks, "So you don't
believe I was in the Spanish Civil War?"

"Good God no! You're not the type."

"What type is that?"

"Political types. Men that are itching for a fight. And
that's not you."

"What if I was in the war? Just for a few months and I don't remember."

"Take it from me you weren't in the war and you are too young to have been in the Great War so end of discussion."

"But I've forgotten so much."

"No, you haven't. You haven't forgotten how to make love to a woman."

"Y...you had to help me."

"Just to get you started that was all." Vere fishes a cigarette out of her pocket and John lights it with one easy movement.

"But I don't think I've done it before the other night."

"What?" Vere asks, coughing in surprise, unaware that John has gone pale. She notices instead that the tennis match has come to an end.

Celeste has allowed Roger to win and he is smiling happily and shaking her hand over the net. John stands up, disorientated; Vere remains seated, shielding her eyes from the sudden glare which is like a spotlight on this small part of Cremorne. Behind a gum tree, Bernard gazes sadly at John. He doesn't join them. Slowly he puts his hands in the pockets of his white trousers and walks off back to the house.

Suddenly something disturbs John. It seems to be the sunlight that is flashing in and out of the trees. He gets up without a word and begins to walk down a path towards the harbour. Vere decides not to stop him. From above Bernard stops walking to watch John's progress. He follows at a safe distance.

While this has been happening, Celeste has gone back to the house and Roger now approaches Vere who has remained seated on the wooden bench near the court. He nods in the direction of Celeste who is nearing the house. Sitting down he says, "She wanted to play first thing this morning but I wouldn't have it."

"Testing you, I expect. Knowing full well you had a massive hangover." Vere pauses. "She's not a pushover you know."

"Oh, I know that. I've been trying to work them out since I got here."

"Who?"

Roger lights a cigarette but doesn't offer one to Vere. "Are you being funny? Celeste and Bernard. Our house masters. They make quite a team."

"I've noticed. I get the feeling they've been doing this for a long time."

"I think they have too."

Vere is scrutinising Roger. "Don't tell me there is a brain under all that bluster?"

"I just want to get the hell out of here!"

"And all your bluster certainly hasn't achieved that."

"I know. I know." Roger sighs heavily. "I'm just sick and tired of sitting around doing nothing."

"I'm going to ask the obvious, Roger."

Roger sighs again. "And what is that?"

"Why don't you do something constructive?"

"Like what?"

Vere can't keep the sarcasm from her voice. "Oh, I don't know. Find out more about our hosts." Vere waits until Roger is looking straight at her. "Seduce Celeste, for instance."

"I might not be your favourite person, as you have told me more than once but when it comes to women I know when I'm in or not."

Vere grimaces. "I suppose the odd one or two might find you..." Vere searches for a suitable word. "Interesting."

"Exciting," Roger says.

Vere bursts out laughing. "Don't flatter yourself."

Roger bites his lip at her reply. "John's interesting, is he? Never thought you'd be one for younger men."

Vere shifts slightly in her seat. "He's surprising."

"You don't fool me."

"I don't care whether I do or not."

Roger stands up to leave. "Have it your way."

Vere chastises herself. This was not going the way she had

planned. In a softer tone she tells him, "As I said, why don't you make yourself useful?" Vere retrieves a cigarette from her pocket, her last she realises. She has forgotten her lighter; Roger doesn't offer to light it, so she is forced to sit there holding it. She's damn well not going to put it back in her pocket.

Roger is nonplussed. "So, what do you suggest?"

"Start digging with Bernard. Man to man."

"For what?"

"Dig into his past. Does he have a wife? Did he fight in the Great War? He's about the right age."

Roger has begun pacing around in small circles near the bench. He stops and stares at Vere. "I just might."

She watches him leave, biding her time until he reaches the house. What an arrogant bastard. As she gets up to leave, she spots John to the right of the house. He is below the terrace standing in the middle of a small clearing. He appears to be looking around him intently. She frowns but doesn't go after him. Instead, she walks slowly back to the house.

The Past

Celeste is uncharacteristically flustered. In a frantic mood she goes through Bernard's bedside table in her room and finds nothing. Moving swiftly, she walks through the connecting door to Bernard's room and begins to go through his writing bureau. After a moment she discovers what looks like an old telegram and reads it carefully.

Of course. Why didn't she anticipate this? Tears spring to her eyes; she brushes them away with unsteady hands. Celeste stands still for a moment, completely at a loss and then spots the photograph pushed to the rear of the bureau. She pockets the telegram and the photograph of a young man and heads for the connecting door.

*

A little while later in Blythe's bedroom, Celeste picks up the baby.

"What are we to do, darling? Tell me what to do."

The baby stares placidly at Celeste.

*

An hour later the last of the sunlight is a swathe of marmalade turning all the houses into storybook versions of themselves. Appearances can be deceiving the houses seem to say. Soon darkness will fall and the quiet street above the bay will be transformed again.

Celeste is standing by a pathway near a street sign that says Kareela Road. She is not far from the Hermitage, but she might as well be light years away. Across the road an abandoned house is being demolished; closer to the house stands the familiar figure of Bernard Halliday. Celeste doesn't wait for him to turn around. Instead, she pulls her coat tightly about her and walks off.

* * *

Pre-dinner Drinks

The grandfather clock in the hall strikes the hour of six as Bernard and Roger sit drinking whiskies in the sitting room. Daphne is asleep at Bernard's feet.

'Where are the girls?" Roger asks.

"Unfortunately, Celeste is not feeling well, so she won't be coming in to dinner. I'm not sure where Vere is. Sketching, I think." Bernard takes a puff of his cigar. "I saw her walk off into the bush below the tennis court with her sketch pad a couple of hours ago."

As Roger lights his cigarette with the lighter from the table, he takes a quick, unobserved glance at Bernard. "What do you make of John?" he asks after sitting back down.

Bernard crosses his legs. "What do mean? He's a pleasant young man. Just lacks confidence."

"There's something not right about him."

"Not right? That's a bit strong, my boy."

"He's the one you should be 'my boying'." Roger emphasises the two words. "Sometimes you'd think he was only about seventeen. Some of the things he says and the way he speaks." Roger hesitates. "He's sort of..." Roger pauses again. Other-worldly."

"The supernatural?" Bernard chuckles. "Fascinating stuff, isn't it?"

"That's not what I mean. I meant..." Roger rubs his forehead, struggling for the right words. "Not of this time. Not the kind of man you encounter now. God, at least I don't. He reminds me of my father."

"He's just a polite young man. And I'm guessing he doesn't move in your social circles."

"You can say that again. What Vere sees in him, is beyond me."

"Yes, it probably is," Bernard remarks faintly. He stubs out his cigar, stands up and goes to the bay window. The harbour is luminous with a gentle orange light, lambent on the water and on the rooftops of several houses below the Hermitage. Bernard watches as it dulls quickly, almost as if it had never been there. He hopes Vere managed to finish her sketch. At that moment, John arrives and sits down a little away from both men.

Bernard finds himself suddenly protective of John. Celeste was right, of course. He must spend more time with John. "How is it going, John?" Bernard asks, sitting back down. "You're looking more rested than this morning."

"Yes, I am thank you." His stutter is only slight this evening. "I was looking for Vere. Do you know where she is?"

"Off sketching somewhere," Roger says. "Evidently."

"Oh. Yes. Well, it is a beautiful sunset."

"It was," Bernard says.

"Do you want a game of tennis tomorrow morning?" Roger asks.

"I don't think I'm much of a player."

Bernard turns away and grimaces.

"Well, we'll soon find out," Roger says with enthusiasm.

They are all going to be in for it, Bernard realises, particularly with Roger's next remark which surprises him.

"Bernard and I had a little discussion about the Great War earlier today." Roger says, reaching for another cigarette. "Or, I should say, Bernard danced rather nimbly around the discussion."

"Dear boy, I didn't know you were so observant of other people."

Roger smiles as at a clever chess move. "My self-centredness is actually a brilliant disguise. It's very useful in business dealings as well. I'm really a snake in the grass."

"A noisy snake," Bernard replies, feeling ill at ease.

"Yes, but I don't miss much."

Mrs Jenkins sounds the gong for dinner and the three men move into the dining room.

* * *

The War

It is after 9 o'clock and Celeste is already in bed and obviously not feeling very well. Her complexion is paler than usual and the skin around her eyes is red. Bernard begins to undress, deciding not to comment on the fact that Celeste has been crying.

Changing tack he remarks, "Vere has been out sketching."

"Did she miss dinner?"

"Yes, but Mrs. Jenkins gave her something. She's been doing some marvellous work."

"How do you know?" Celeste sits up slightly in bed.

"I took a peek."

"I'm pleased."

"That's the good news."

Celeste sighs. "And the bad?"

"Our dear Roger has stopped his tantrums and changed tack. He's now conducting his own investigations."

"Vere's idea?"

"Probably."

"Oh no! On what?"

"On the war in the afternoon and me. And on John in the evening."

"On you?"

"Yes. My war service or lack thereof. I said I didn't serve. My lungs, you know."

"And did he believe you?"

"I don't think so."

"Has he had a chance to really talk to Vere?"

Bernard rubs his eyes in tiredness. "I'm not sure. But we're not going to be able to keep them apart."

"I know."

"And there's another problem."

"What now?" Celeste asks tiredly.

"Roger has invited John to a game of tennis."

Celeste sighs like someone who has given up the fight. "Well, we knew it would happen like we feared but it's the fifth day tomorrow, not the second. So, we should be thankful for that. You said it was inevitable remember."

"Yes, I did," Bernard says.

"And things have to be worked through."

Bernard glances at her face. "Can I ask why you have been crying?"

"No, you can't." Quickly she adds, "What did John say when Roger asked him. He didn't seem to remember anything when he was watching my game today."

"He said he didn't think he was much of a player."

"Oh, poor darling."

"Quite," Bernard says turning out his night lamp. Celeste turns out hers, wiping more tears from her eyes.

* * *

THE FIFTH DAY

Another Game

Vere and Bernard are not at the tennis court; there is only Celeste watching the game. Suddenly John makes a stunning lob and Roger throws down his racket in disgust. Mimicking John's soft manner of speech he says, "I'm not much of a player. I'm not much of a player, my ass!" Roger groans and turns towards Celeste on the bench who is keeping score. "How many points have I got off him in seven games?"

"Two."

"Two fucking points! I know enough about tennis to spot a professional player when I see one and why the fuck haven't I heard of you?" he asks, swinging around to face John. "I go to a lot of the matches at White City and I've never seen you play."

"I'm not sure."

"You're not sure. God, you don't know much do you,

102

mate? You've forgotten just about everything including the fact that you are a professional tennis player!"

"He hasn't been well, Roger and he doesn't need you attacking him," Celeste says.

"Of course not! We mustn't attack John. We mustn't try and jog his memory."

"I don't know about you boys, but I really need a cup of tea."

"Diversionary tactics again. You and Bernard are certainly experts. The perfect hosts who don't want their guests asking too many questions."

"That's enough, Roger," Celeste says, leaving the bench.

"And John." Roger picks up his racquet and waves it in Celeste's direction. "Never mind that he's wearing clothes from twenty years ago. We are just supposed to ignore that. And," Roger drags the word out, "just accept the fact that he's forgotten he's a professional tennis player." Roger wipes sweat off his forehead. "And another tiny fact. None of us can leave! But this is the Hermitage. We are here to rest and recuperate and have a relaxing week."

"Please don't speak to Celeste like that," John says, collecting the spare rackets.

"Always so polite. Don't you wonder in that fog of a brain of yours, why you are different from the rest of us?"

Celeste is now at the gate in the fence. She opens it and says to John who is the nearest, "Come with me, John. He's a bad sport and he doesn't like being beaten." She places a hand on John as he leaves the court. "You played beautifully."

Roger is behind them, still on the court and glaring at their backs as they leave.

"Why did I play like that?" John asks, as they walk towards the house.

Celeste doesn't answer but carefully leads him to the back of the house near the azaleas and the laundry. They reach an area screened by lattice when suddenly John bends over in pain.

Celeste is alarmed. "John!" She steers him to a wooden

bench where they both sit down.

"It's the back of my neck. Why does it keep hurting like this?"

At that moment Vere arrives. "Mrs Jenkins said I would find you here." Vere stands by the bench. "John, what is the matter?"

Celeste gets up from the bench. "It's his head again. I'll leave him in your care."

Vere frowns as Celeste quickly leaves. She doesn't notice that there are tears in Celeste's eyes. After a moment Vere pulls John's head up to look into his eyes. He refuses to meet her gaze and tries to push her away.

"You don't get rid of me that easy." When John doesn't answer she asks, "Did I hear Roger shouting again?" She sighs. "But then he's always shouting so there's probably nothing to worry about."

John finally looks at Vere. "There is."

"What?"

"Something to worry about."

"Is there? Let me be the judge of that." Vere pulls him up. They both stand for a moment.

John is still unsteady on his feet and Vere waits for him to regain a measure of control. As they move off towards the back door that leads to the kitchen, John suddenly speaks. "I don't know who I am. Not at all."

"You're my lover, that's who you are," Vere tells him, as they encounter Mrs Jenkins in the kitchen making pastry. Vere smiles at Mrs Jenkins who smiles pleasantly back. She then leads John to her bedroom and closes the door.

* * *

Aftermath

Later in the afternoon, Celeste hurries into the sitting room.
Bernard frowns at her slightly flustered state.

He puts his journal down and says, "Are you looking for
Roger, C? My dear, it sounded like he was being exceedingly
unpleasant even by his standards. I could hear him from here this
morning."

"So, where is he?" Celeste asks sharply.

"He's gone for a walk again. A long one he informed me
when he left. He was muttering something about reaching
Cremorne Wharf, if it was the last thing he did." Bernard smiles
to himself. "Well, of course it won't be the last thing he did."
Bernard glances up at Celeste who is still standing in front of
him. "Some of them do put up such a fight."

With his reply, Celeste stares down at Bernard in a
determined manner, very unlike her usual, calm self. She speaks
slowly, emphasising each word. "I can't take this anymore."

Bernard studies her more closely. "My dear, I know he is one of our worst but we will sort him out."

"I'm not talking about Roger."

Bernard moves forward in his seat. "Then, what are you talking about, C?"

"I'm talking about you."

"Me? I am my usual self." He hesitates. "Why don't you sit down, my dear?"

"No, I won't sit down and no, you are not your usual self. You haven't been for days. Not since John arrived actually."

Bernard motions her to come close but she steps back. Her movement away from him disconcerts Bernard. "I don't know what you are talking about."

"I saw you at Kareela Road watching your house being demolished."

"Trying to catch me out my dear, sweet Celeste? Well, it won't work." Suddenly Bernard speaks in parrot fashion. "They will demolish the house; they are demolishing the house and they have demolished the house and so it goes on."

"Then it shouldn't worry you but it obviously does."

Bernard doesn't answer immediately, he merely folds his illustrated journal in half and stands up.

Face to face, Celeste is half a head taller than him. "Just as I thought," Celeste says softly.

Bernard moves towards her in a threatening manner. "You have no idea what you are talking about."

Celeste stands her ground. "Haven't I? It's obvious now. So obvious that you are not a host anymore." Celeste stumbles over the last few words.

Bernard takes the opportunity to change tack and speaks to her soothingly. "Don't be absurd, C. You're just tired. Our darling Roger has worn you out."

"Don't patronise me, Bernard. I am not stupid. I know exactly what is happening." Celeste begins walking around the room in an endeavour to keep her composure.

Bernard sits back down. "And what is that, my dear?"

Celeste stops by the bay window. She stays there for a few minutes watching a ferry chug slowly past. Unable to face him she says to the view, "Oh Bernard, you are not a host anymore. You are a guest and you are now facing your worst fear with John." Celeste rubs her forehead wearily and moves towards the centre of the room, the low table separating them.

"You are just like them. You've never let go of the past. I don't know why I didn't see it till now. Especially when I consider what happened to you." She says even more gently. "I thought you were different but I was wrong. And to think you chose the same way out as Roger." Celeste pauses. "A length of rope."

Bernard raises his head to meet Celeste's eyes. "Simply cause and effect, my dear. My darling boy died and I saw no reason to continue living."

"Exactly. And you've never come to terms with it. So, I guess it's you that's leaving, not me! I'm not going anywhere. I've decided to continue to host more groups after you've gone."

Bernard picks up his journal again and opens it. "We'll see."

Celeste moves quickly around the table, grabs the illustrated paper off Bernard and throws it on the carpet. "You are not in a fit state. You're leaving with John. You are helping John by accompanying him, just as you couldn't help Byron."

Before Bernard can get up from his chair, Celeste throws her arms around him and leans her cheek against the top of his head. "They were in the same battalion, weren't they? Seven of them marched away from the others and shot in the back of the neck."

Bernard shoves Celeste; she narrowly misses falling on the table. "Shut up! Shut up!"

The silence between them is terrible. Finally, Celeste says, "You need to go with him. He just needs someone to go with him."

* * *

THE SIXTH DAY

Last things

In Vere's room the curtains have been closed against the
morning sun. John sits in bed resting against two pillows
propped up behind him. He is naked to the waist and looks tired.
Vere, wearing a beautiful oyster coloured slip, sits crossed-
legged facing him. She has her hand on his leg under the covers.

John rubs the back of his neck. "You didn't let me finish."

"You're being absurd, John. You are not dead!" She leans
towards him and says in a softer tone. "The same could not be
said for some of my other beaus. Lifeless. As for you." She
smiles at him. "You have been quite a treat."

"Please don't speak about our lovemaking like that."

"Lovemaking? Oh God, you are a schoolboy sometimes."

"Well, I can't help it."

"I know you can't." Vere touches his face tenderly.

John grabs her hand. "I've started to remember things. So now I know."

To hide her alarm Vere jumps off the bed to light herself a cigarette. She offers it to John before she smokes it. "You are not dead."

"Just one puff." As he takes the cigarette from her, he decides to play along with Vere. "Well, if I'm not dead, what's your theory about all my missing years and my clothes. I mean I'm the only one missing about twenty-five years." Vere frowns so he continues. "You and Roger have only lost a few weeks. Well, you a few weeks. Roger hasn't said anything about missing any time."

"Yes, but I get the feeling he's confused about that development of his. He's not sure if it went through or not. I think he's hazy too. He just won't admit it. He's working on Bernard now and he seems to be getting under his skin."

"He is. Bernard was very quiet at dinner last night."

"Was he?"

"Yes. So, what is your theory." John smiles wearily at Vere.

Vere straightens her back and smokes her cigarette. "Let's look at all the players in this mystery."

"All right."

"If we look at Bernard and Celeste as time travellers then it sort of makes sense. What if they decide to regularly have guests?"

"What?"

"Just wait. Maybe the house or even the ferry are the way they travel. We know they've been to 1945 or even later than that." Vere pauses. "I'm going to check her room again for more books with interesting dates."

"I'm confused."

"Sorry. Say, they are from 1955 or later. They like to go back in time and have guests at this house to keep them company. They invite people that need a break. Like me and Roger. I was fed up with work and hadn't had a holiday in years.

Roger was obviously stressed and overworked."

"But what about me? I don't fit in."

"Well, you do. You've been sick. I just think something went wrong when you arrived.

"Maybe it was when I got on the ferry."

Excitement sweeps Vere along. "Yes. That's it. Maybe you shouldn't have got on our ferry. They were playing 1937 and you got on by mistake. Maybe you should have got, say, the next ferry which would have been some guests from maybe, 1912 or thereabouts."

"I didn't feel right on the ferry. Everything looked different."

"Yes, I remember. If say, someone else from 1937 had got on instead of you then things wouldn't have got so bad, so quickly."

"But what about Roger? He's been so difficult, hasn't he?"

"Oh yes, he's definitely made things worse with his bloody-mindedness. And his walks! Perhaps other guests never

115

realised they couldn't leave."

John looks at Vere tenderly. "And you noticed her dress and became suspicious."

Vere nods her head. "Yes, and we've got you from the wrong time with your tennis playing."

"And Roger insisting we use the court."

"Thinking back, they were annoyed about that but what could they do?"

"They were. But that doesn't explain my neck."

Vere leans forward touching John's legs again. "Yes, it does. You've had some sort of injury and then you had to have time off work."

"And somehow when I came here, I lost twenty-five years."

"Yes. That's it."

"But they didn't seem surprised to see me."

"Damn," Vere says, pausing to think. "But wait. It was Bernard who met us first, wasn't it?"

"Yes."

"He's a sly dog. He has a real poker face. He could have been surprised but hid it well."

John is trying to remember. "Possibly."

Vere runs her hands through her unruly hair. "Yes, that's it. I mean they were expecting you soon but not on that ferry trip."

John speaks slowly. "I see what you mean. It's just I have these strange dreams, feelings of being in danger."

Vere moves closer to sit on his lap, her legs tucked under her, either side of his body. "I'm guessing you had some sort of accident. Maybe something fell on you in the street or something. That's why you yell out about getting down. You tried to warn people before you got hurt."

At that moment John seems to remember something but he pushes the thought aside. Instead, he takes Vere's face in his hands and kisses her gently. She is taken aback by his sudden tenderness. She tries to move away but he holds her tight. After a

117

moment she begins to relax in his arms and kisses him

passionately back.

*

In Celeste's room mid-afternoon, Vere moves silently about the

room checking the books on a small bookshelf and by Celeste's

bed. She puts them back quickly. They are ones she has seen

before. Something makes her check behind the window seat. She

pushes aside the dark ticket curtain and finds a large book,

partially hidden under a pale pink cushion. She picks it up.

"Such a big soft book," Vere says to herself, gasping when she

sees the date. "1984." She turns at the sound of movement

behind her. It is Celeste looking at her with a strange, sad

expression on her face.

Celeste walks towards her. "I think I should tell you, Vere.

John is dead. I'm so sorry."

"Dead. No!" Vere begins to sob. "Just now?"

118

"No, not now. A long time ago."

"Oh no." Vere struggles not to cry. After a long moment she rubs at her face and straightens up. Then I must be too."

"Yes."

"How?"

"You were rushing, getting off the Bourke Street tram."

"Oh God!"

Vere collapses in distress and Celeste gently leads her to the window seat, where she sobs hysterically. She is still crying softly when Celeste, standing next to her, begins to stroke her shoulder. Vere is facing the window. Outside the harbour is glorious with several yachts close by. Oh, to be on one of them, Vere wishes. "And Roger?" she asks finally.

"You don't need to worry about Roger. But he is dead too."

"How did John die?

For a moment Celeste doesn't answer. Instead, she too watches the harbour and the yachts. Sighing she says, "That doesn't matter now. He loves you and you will wait for him."

"What do you mean?"

"For the first time in your life someone loves you."

Celeste closes her eyes for a moment. I can't imagine having a
mother who didn't love me. And no father."

"It was my life. But what do you mean about me waiting?"

"You are leaving. And then you need to wait for John.
Take the book with you. Here. There's a nice spot to read on the
bench under the yew tree hedge. Do you know it? It is near the
kitchen garden."

"Yes."

"Can I stay here on the window seat for a bit? I don't want
to see anyone for a while."

"Yes, of course."

Celeste leaves the room, closing the door softly.

Vere brings her legs up on to the window seat and pulls
the curtains across, cutting off the rest of the world. She picks up
the book again and looks at the title. "The Name of the Rose by

Umberto Eco," she whispers to herself, hugging the book.

*

In Blythe's bedroom, the baby is stirring in her cot. Celeste leans over stroking Blythe's leg.

"Do you miss Mummy? I do. God, I wish she was here. She could sort out this unholy mess." Carefully Celeste takes Byron's photograph from her pocket and studies it again.

"What to do?" she asks Blythe. "What to do, my darling."

*

It is now late afternoon and Vere is sitting in the bath with a razor. She takes it and puts it against her left wrist. She is sobbing and then laughs raggedly as she remembers something. She throws the razor to the bathroom floor as the grandfather clock strikes the hour of five. Moments later there is a loud knocking on the door.

"Please, Vere. Open the door. I need to speak to you now."

"I've just had a bath, John. Please let me get dressed."

John listens as the bathwater sloshes and then gurgles away. "All right," he says after a moment.

"Can you look for my shoes? I'll get dressed in here. I've brought a change of clothes."

John and Vere meet in the hall shortly after. He hands Vere her shoes.

"I love you, you silly goose. I'm just going to sit outside for a little while. Give me five minutes, would you?"

John nods. He is too upset to speak.

"And then come and get me," Vere calls down the hall as she heads for her room. "I thought we could go for a walk. I think it's going to be a beautiful sunset." Leaving John standing puzzled in the hall, Vere runs to her room, dumps her towel and dirty clothes and still barefoot, carrying her shoes, she heads to the kitchen.

"Hello, Mrs Jenkins. I'm going to sit outside for a bit."

"That's a good idea, love."

Vere puts her shoes on and wanders through the small paths that intersect the vegetable garden. She smiles at the lettuces, beans, spring onions and carrots and other vegetables and herbs she can't identify. As she walks through the garden the sunlight follows her path and falls ahead on the stone bench, turning it from a dull grey brown to a golden biscuit colour. She sits down on it and throws her head back in relief; the last rays of the sun warming her face. She watches the clouds race across the sky and then closes her eyes.

* * *

Evening

Celeste is sitting on the bench under the yew tree hedge with Blythe. The sun has set and the back garden is illuminated by the light in the kitchen and a small green lantern hanging near the back door. Mrs Jenkins is doing the dishes and a magpie is calling the evening on.

"Round and round the garden like a teddy bear. One step..." Suddenly Celeste gasps. "Roger! Did you just get back?"

Roger stops in front of them and bends over trying to catch his breath. It takes him a moment to speak. "Yes, I know. I'm a complete idiot."

"Here. Sit down on the bench with us." Celeste makes room for him.

"And how are you, Madam?" Roger asks, facing Blythe who makes talking noises at him. "She's very knowing, isn't she? What do they say about babies like Blythe?"

"That's she's been here before?"

"She certainly is an unusual baby," Roger says.

"I know."

"How many of us for dinner tonight?"

"I'm not sure."

"Bernard? Are we stuck with the old bastard tonight?"

Celeste raises her eyebrows at the question. It has been a trying few hours and there is still so much to do. She struggles to keep her voice calm. "I don't think we will be. Nor Vere."

Roger is silent for a moment. "Where has our darling Vere gone? Off sketching again? I hope she's taken a hurricane lamp with her."

"No, she won't be needing that. She's left the Hermitage."

Roger is flabbergasted. "What do you mean left? I thought none of us can leave!"

"Not until certain things have been worked out."

"And what did Vere work out?" Roger asks. He is determined to remain angry and frustrated but this is proving difficult with a beautiful baby staring at him wide-eyed. She is wearing a dainty pink dress with a matching cardigan and only socks on her feet. She reaches across to touch his hair.

Roger takes her tiny hand, feeling as he does so a calming stillness wash over him.

"Now that would be telling," Celeste says, watching the baby and Roger.

"Right. And what have I got to work out?"

"I can't say."

"Jesus, fucking Christ! I'm sick of this place."

The baby frowns at the outburst but doesn't pull her hand away.

"Perhaps patience is required, do you think? In your case, I mean," Celeste says gently.

"Another tick off from my dear, sweet hostess."

"I'm sorry you feel like that."

"So, it's like some weird parlour game?"

Celeste pauses for a moment, frowning. "Yes, I suppose it is. I hadn't thought of it quite like that. But what a brilliant metaphor for life. A weird parlour game. There are people in our lives and then suddenly they are gone." Celeste hesitates, studying Roger in the half light. "I have a lot to do and I can't do it with Blythe. Could you bring her inside, in say fifteen minutes?"

Roger decides he doesn't mind. What the hell. "All right, Celeste. Blythe and I will talk about current world events, the economy, wool prices."

"And she's dining with us," Celeste says, handing the baby over.

"What joy," Roger says as Celeste walks towards the kitchen. He then settles the baby in his lap and whispers to her, "We can discuss the menu."

The light from the hanging lantern falls softly on the head of the man and the small child, forming halos that would alarm Celeste to see. Before long Roger begins to sing a song about bluebirds flying away for Blythe, who is intently watching Roger's fingers as he opens each one individually and then closes them again, using small pieces of paper from his pocket to imitate the birds.

*

Celeste rushes to the library where a distressed John is pacing up and down. "I've looked everywhere for her. Everywhere. You need to tell me where she is!"

"John, please calm yourself. She's gone but you will be with her soon."

"What do you mean. Just like that? Why can't I be with her right now?"

Celeste grabs both his hands to stop him pacing. "You need to do something for me first and then you will see Vere."

"What? What do I need to do? I don't understand." John runs his hands through his hair. He is almost as distraught as on the night of the storm.

"You need to talk to Bernard about his son Byron."

128

Celeste takes a deep breath. "You were with Byron when you died."

John sits down suddenly on the couch. "Then I am dead? Vere said you and Bernard were time travellers."

Celeste sits down next to him. "She was partly right but not completely."

"So, she's gone because she worked out what's happening here? What this place is really about." John searches Celeste's expression for a reply.

"No, John. She worked something else out. That's why she's gone."

"What?" John asks, becoming distressed again.

"It's not for me to say. Here, John." Celeste takes something out of the pocket in her skirt. "It's a photograph of Byron. He was in your battalion. Do you recognise him?"

"Yes, that's Captain Montgomery."

"So you do remember the war?"

"Yes. The last day or so," John says, not meeting Celeste's

eyes. "I only know that we seemed to be marching forever. I'm not sure how many of us there were. Probably only seven or so and less of the Krauts but we were just too tired to take them and we were almost out of ammunition." John shudders at the memory but he continues speaking.

"We thought they were marching us to some sort of base camp where we'd be prisoners of war, but I had this awful feeling of inevitability, sort of like drowning, that we weren't going to get out of it. I was immediately behind Byron and I could tell that he felt the same way. He kept trying to gee-up the younger ones following behind us. He'd yell back encouragement but the second time they jabbed him in the guts with a rifle butt for his troubles."

Celeste quickly wipes tears from her eyes before John notices and squeezes his hand to go on.

"That's all I remember. Soon after they lined us up. And then there was this terrible pain in the back of my neck."

"I'm so sorry, John," Celeste says. "You didn't tell Vere

any of this?"

"No. I didn't want to upset her. She was trying so hard to piece everything together."

"She loved you. She really did. And now it's your turn to go, but I need your help first."

John lifts his head to face Celeste. "He was a wonderful captain. When the Krauts lined us up he said, 'I'm with you boys. Hold your heads high.' John begins to sob. "And we did."

 Celeste puts her arms around John until he stops crying. After a moment she says, "Please. Can you tell that to Bernard?"

"But why?"

"Because Byron Montgomery was Bernard's only child."

"But I thought he was Bernard Halliday not Montgomery."

"Halliday is just a name Bernard likes to use when he's staying at the Hermitage."

"Oh."

"Can you tell him, John?"

"But he's not here, is he?"

"He's not far away. At number 72 Kareela Road near Hodgson Avenue."

"But I thought we couldn't leave."

"You'll be able to find the place easily. It has just been demolished." When John still looks unsure, she says, "This is very important." Celeste stands up and smiles reassuringly at John. "Now I must get back to Blythe. Could you take Daphne with you? She needs a walk."

*

A wind has risen and the pines behind the house are whispering. Blythe's mobile is tinkling, Celeste's mantle clock chiming faintly and the grandfather clock is loudly counting off the time with six gongs.

In the kitchen every surface has been scrubbed and Mrs Jenkins is washing up the last pot when Celeste bursts into the room. She is panting and disorientated. "Blythe's gone. Roger

132

has taken her! I wanted to say goodbye to her." Celeste sobs the last few words.

Mrs Jenkins finishes wiping up the last pot, hangs up her tea towel and moves towards Celeste. "You mean Blythe has taken Roger."

"No! Why would you say that?"

"You know it's true. Roger just needed a bit of peace and quiet. Some calm. Blythe gave him that."

"But I wanted to leave with Blythe."

"I thought you told Bernard you were staying."

"I was only bluffing and now everything has happened so fast. Why has it all happened so fast this time?"

"You know it sometimes does, my dear."

"They have gone, haven't they?" Celeste asks, looking about the kitchen.

"Bernard, John and the dog have gone. And the others before them of course."

"You knew they were all going, didn't you, because you

haven't cooked any dinner."

"Only a shepherd's pie just in case you were hungry. I put it in the pantry."

"I don't want anything, Mrs Jenkins."

"For heaven's sake call me Ethel."

Gazing out into the twilight, Celeste says again, "I wanted to leave with Blythe; Now who shall I leave with?"

"Funny you should say that." Mrs Jenkins remarks.

* * * * *

Debbie Robson loves to write fiction set in the first sixty years of the last century. She has had stories published in Serious Flash, The Viridian Door, Bombay Lit Mag and others and poetry in Emerge Journal, The Martello Journal, The Passionfruit Review and more. She tweets @lakelady2282

Made in the USA
Middletown, DE
10 November 2023

42182641R00076